Disturbing
the
Peace

WINONA KENT

Print ISBN: 978-0-9880826-4-9
eBook ISBN: 978-0-9880826-3-2:

Please visit Winona's website at www.winonakent.com

Also by Winona Kent:

Marianne's Memory
In Loving Memory
Perhaps an Angel
Persistence of Memory
Cold Play
The Cilla Rose Affair
Skywatcher

.

PART ONE

It was a dream come true for me.

A regular spot at The Blue Devil Club, playing guitar in a four-piece jazz combo, my three mates on tenor sax, organ and drums. I needed to be good to gig with them, and I was. I'd practised on board the *Star Sapphire* as a guest musician. And after leaving the sea, I'd honed my talent and skills in Hong Kong, and then Australia. By the time I landed back in London, my itchy feet tempered (for the moment, anyway) I was ready.

We support the main show and the one after-hours, and from time to time we're part of the headliner's line-up.

I'm often wandering off home in a taxi just as everyone else is waking up...the birds sending out experimental morning chirps ahead of sunrise, trains and buses and early cars making their first appearances of the day. I leave my guitars at work— my flat on Pentonville Road is cruise-ship-cabin small. I think that's what made it appealing. But there's barely room for my clothes, a nice comfy bed and an equally comfy sofa, let alone show-off space for two solid body Fenders (a Tele and a Strat), a handsome black Phoenix hollow-body—Brian Setzer plays one—and a lovely Gibson ES-175, an archtop, a favourite of traditionalists, though I find it uncomfortable because of an old injury from my *Sapphire* days.

It was a chilly night in January when my son came to see me. He rang ahead to let me know he'd be there, so I arranged a decent table for him, plus a meal and some drinks. And a bed for the night at my flat. Dom's at college now, studying film production. He lives with my mum, close enough to London that he can catch a train in every morning. Far enough away that trekking home at that hour of the night wasn't an option.

My mum's getting on in years but she looked after Dom when I ran away to sea after Emma died. And the arrangement's stuck.

"Did you enjoy it?" I asked, outside, desperate for a smoke and hunting for a taxi. It was past three in the morning.

"I did," he said. "Not my kind of music. But nonetheless interesting within the context of musical divergency."

He speaks like that now. College has done unforgivable things to his vocabulary.

"I'm going to make a film," he added. "A documentary. Part of my coursework."

"About me?" I asked, foolishly, lighting up.

"About Ben Quigley."

Ben Quigley. Played rhythm guitar for Figgis Green in the late-1960s. He'd disappeared from radar four years earlier.

"Why Ben?"

"He's a legend," Dom shrugged. "The quiet guy in the back. And nobody seems to know what happened to him. I'd like to find out."

I'd had this driver many times before. He's from Lucknow and he's fond of a late-night chat. "Angel?" he checked, though it's never not.

"Angel," I confirmed, stubbing out my cigarette on the wet pavement.

"Anyway, I thought you might be able to help," Dom said, as we climbed into the taxi.

I'm the de facto archivist for Figgis Green. My mum is Mandy Green, the source of one half of the group's name. The source of the other half was my dad, Tony Figgis. If anyone wants to know anything about the band—its history, obscure details like my dad's first instrument (it was the piano—when he was thirteen he passed the entrance exams at Trinity Music College in London) or where my mum got her stage clothes (they were created by a fashion design student named Liz), whatever happened to so and so (he's running a pub in Epsom)—they ask me. I'm in touch with everyone who ever played with the band. The guy on bass was mum's brother. The drummer was dad's cousin. And the fellow who played fiddle ended up producing records. Ben Quigley was the only one I'd ever managed to misplace.

And my son was right. He was a legend.

"Have you tried the police?"

"I have," said Dom, "but there's no missing person's file, so they're not much use."

"What's triggered your inquiring mind?"

"Sophie's sister's got a job at the bank where he has his accounts."

Sophie's his current girlfriend. Her sister's a temp. She once worked for a guy who went to prison for embezzlement.

"Nothing's been touched since 2013."

"I'm not sure how useful I can be."

"You know people in the music business. They'll open their doors to you. You can ask the right sorts of questions. Perhaps jog some memories."

"He could be dead," I said.

"He could be," Dom replied. "But I'd prefer to believe that he's not. And when are you going to stop smoking?"

#

I was a smoker before Emma died. And then I gave it up. A discarded cigarette caused the fire that took her life, and I'd assumed the blame. In the end, it turned out not to be my fault at all.

I stayed away from cigarettes for about five years, and then I started again. My preferred poison these days is Benson and Hedges Gold. I'd be lying if I said I didn't want to stop. I do. But my willpower is weaker than my intent.

Ben was a smoker too.

I knew he was missing in action. I'd followed his story, the same way I'd followed Gerry Rafferty's: with a sinking heart and not much optimism, knowing how musical souls could be battered like the sea crashing up onto Hebridean rocks in a gale.

Gerry Rafferty was ravaged by drink. He'd checked into a five star hotel and trashed his room. A friend had paid his bill and taken him to hospital, but then he'd discharged himself, leaving behind all of his personal belongings. A missing person's report was never filed with the police. After that, he'd gone to ground…a spokesman said he was in the south of England, being cared for by a friend…a solicitor issued a statement that he was in Tuscany, working on a new album. In truth he was living with the love of his life in Dorset, where his body ultimately surrendered to the devastation of his addiction.

Ben Quigley's life was similar to Gerry Rafferty's, but without the six haunting minutes of *Baker Street*. He was a sensitive soul, an excessive drinker, a musician who'd shied away from the attention Figgis Green had brought him. He hated touring, hated drawing attention to himself. After Figgis Green had disbanded in the 1970s, he'd made it on his own, spectacularly, his soaring successes interspersed with mind-boggling, headline generating crashes to earth.

Had he gone to ground deliberately four years

ago? Or had something else happened to him?

I thought I'd start with my mum. She's got a mind like a steel trap, in spite of her advancing years.

"The last time I saw him was six...no, it was seven years ago, dear." She slid an ashtray towards me at the kitchen table. She knows me too well. "It was at the funeral of his daughter. You weren't here—you'd just begun to work at sea. I thought I'd best go along and pay my respects. There weren't many others there. Ben was very pleased to see me. He asked about you and Angie."

Angie's my sister. She writes best-selling mysteries under a pseudonym. Apparently readers are more likely to buy a novel by an author named Taylor Feldspar than one by Angie Figgis.

Ben Quigley's only child passed away at the age of thirty-nine of a drug overdose. She was living rough and had been for years. Her mum also died young, from a rampaging tumour that filled her body with its cancerous evil. Ben didn't marry again.

I'd had a look online, just to reconfirm what I knew about him, and the last time he'd been mentioned anywhere. There really wasn't much. A Wikipedia entry, a stub which was an offshoot from the main entry about Figgis Green. Where he was born—Mitcham—and when—01 May 1941—and how he came to be the group—he was hired in 1968 after the original rhythm guitarist, Rick Redding, was dismissed for untoward behaviour. Specifically, causing grievous bodily harm to my dad.

I was born in 1968 and I had patchy recollections

of meeting Ben a few times while the group was still together. There was one get-together—I think it must have been Christmas because I remember decorations and paper hats and my parents giving me a toy castle with turrets and a real working drawbridge and little warriors in armour and on horseback that I could pit against one another in amazing adventures. I remember it because Ben was there, and rather than mingle with the adults in the lounge, he came upstairs to my bedroom and together we sat on the floor and invented a fantastic battle in the castle.

Kids are natural dreamers. Their imaginations know no bounds. It all gets turned on its head when they go to school and are forced to divert their attention to more mundane things like adding and subtracting and identifying the three different states of water. Ben Quigley was the only adult I'd ever met who had the kind of imagination that I had when I was five. He *was* Sir Lancelot.

"And did Dominic say why he wanted to do a film about him?" my mother inquired, adding, "He doesn't tell me anything."

"He was the quiet guy in the back," I said.

"Quite a change from his predecessor," my mum agreed. "He never did like being in the spotlight. Sometimes I used to wonder if he was actually there. I mean, he was there—he was a perfectly accomplished musician and he was very professional and never missed a cue—but his mind always seemed to be somewhere else."

"Must have driven his teachers mad," I said.

"He did used to say that, yes, dear. He was always in trouble for not paying attention in school. His mother's still alive, you know. Although she's much older than me."

My mum was born in the same year as Ben. A war baby.

"How do you know that?"

"I read about her. Just let me think…where was it now?"

I waited while she went through the process of association and elimination.

"Oh yes, that was it, dear. She'd won a large sum of money in a contest and the local paper had thought it was interesting so they'd sent a reporter and a photographer round to the care home where she was staying and they'd written a story about her."

"Do you remember the name of the care home or where it was?"

"I'm afraid I don't dear, no. Somewhere in London. I was reading it online. I wasn't actually paying attention to the name of the newspaper."

Online. The magical words.

"Edith Quigley," my mum added, helpfully. "She'd be in her 90s."

#

Ninety-six, to be exact. I looked her up on Ancestry. Quigley's an uncommon name, and I didn't have to search too hard. Edith Cross, who married Joseph Quigley sometime in the first three months of 1939 in Surrey Mid-Eastern.

A quick online search for Edith Quigley brought up the local south London newspaper that had reported her contest win and gave me the name of the care home. I was lucky—she was born in Mitcham and she'd married in Mitcham and she'd lived in Mitcham all of her life. I wasn't going to have to travel far to find her.

I took my car. I do drive, though I gave it up when I was at sea, and didn't bother with it when I was living in Hong Kong and Australia. I always think of cars as I would a horse…stabled somewhere nice and clean and warm, all wants and needs taken care of, and regularly taken out for a trot round the track.

My horse is an old silver Volvo V70. It's fast, reliable and tough, and has room for all my gear in the back if I'm playing a gig somewhere that isn't The Blue Devil. I bought it second-hand from the police.

Edith Quigley's home was a little flat in a newish building that offered extra care housing, bingo on Tuesdays, hot meals in the restaurant and a sheltered garden at the back—although it was mid-January and far too chilly and wet to sit outside. It would have been lovely in the summer.

A woman named Maureen took me to see Edith in the residents' lounge. "She's all there," she whispered, confidentially, as we walked through to the big open room where Edith was sitting in her wheelchair, a little tank feeding oxygen through a transparent tube into her nose. "But her mind does wander a bit. I should warn you that she does tend to go off on tangents."

"My grandmother was the same," I said, easily. It was true. From my gran I learned patience and how to listen. And how to gently nudge a meandering memory back into the present.

Ben Quigley's mum was a little bird of a woman, nothing like my gran, who I remembered as comfortable and cushiony and smelling of face powder and lavender. Maureen brought us cups of tea and a plate of chocolate digestives and then, with a cheery wave and a warning about no smoking or open flames, disappeared.

"What did you say your name was?" Edith asked, her voice as tiny as her body.

"Jason Davey," I said, and then I corrected myself. "Jason Figgis." David is my middle name, and I've used Davey professionally for as long as I can remember.

"Oh, Figgis," she said. "Yes. You're Tony's boy, aren't you?"

Maureen was right. Edith was totally on the ball.

"I am."

"Figgis Green was my Benny's favourite band. He enjoyed playing with them."

"I know he did." Time for a gentle nudge. "I'm trying to locate Ben, Edith. And I'm not sure where to start looking. Have you heard from him recently?"

"Oh yes. Quite recently."

Little lights and bells started going off in my mind.

"How recently?"

"I had a letter. It came in the post. Let me think."

I waited.

"No," she said, "it's left me. If you'd like to take me to my room, I could show you the letter."

I wondered about the propriety of wheeling Edith into a private part of the home. Where was Maureen?

I spotted her, offering plates of biscuits to two other elderly residents sitting by the window.

"Would it be all right if I went with Edith to her flat?"

"Yes, of course. I'll be here if you need me."

Edith's room was an open-plan studio affair, with a private loo that had a shower you could walk—or wheel—into, and lots of hand rails. There was a tiny little kitchen in the corner with a microwave and a fridge and a sink—not designed for real cooking, but meals were taken in the restaurant anyway. And the main part of the room had a comfy armchair and a neatly made bed and the sorts of knick-knacks you'd expect from a lifetime of mantelpieces.

"Now where did I put it?" Edith wondered, her eyes darting everywhere. She decided on a large wicker basket beside the bed which seemed to contain a collection of completely unrelated articles: a box of tissues, a package of biscuits, two pairs of reading glasses, a rosary, a pair of scissors, and an A to Z of London from about 1975. As well as the letter from Ben, which she handed to me.

It was still inside its envelope. I looked for a return address but there was nothing written on the front or the back. I checked the postmark. Sent from London. On the 23rd of June 2013.

"Four years ago," I said, to Edith, pulling the single sheet of paper out and glancing over the brief, handwritten scrawl.

"Has it been that long? Dear me."

Hello mum. How are you? Just a quick note to say I'm well. Still playing some concerts here and there. The old fans still remember. And now they're bringing their grandkids. I'm booked to do a music festival next month. Love, Ben xxx

"Did he ring you or write to you at all after this letter?"

"No, he didn't. It was very naughty of him. His father was the same. Just after I married him he was sent off to fight somewhere and he didn't write either. Though of course he likely wasn't allowed to because of the secrecy. He was away more than he was home."

She leaned forward, a little conspiratorially.

"I'm afraid I was very naughty too. I met a handsome Yank soldier while Joe was away and I had a little fling."

I didn't say anything. It happened a lot during the war.

"And that's how Ben got started. My handsome Yank was shipped out and then Joe came home, and we had about a month together and then he was killed in an air raid. So there I was, all alone, and me pregnant with Ben, so I went to live with my aunt and her house had been bombed. They'd put a tarpaulin over a hole in the roof. Two rooms weren't habitable so I slept downstairs on the sofa. When we weren't in the shelter. And my uncle, of course, was an ARP warden so he was out all night. They had a son, my cousin, ever such a lovely young man…"

I didn't like to cut her off. I'd learned, with my gran, that sometimes a wandering mind was just a sign of needing to talk to someone—anyone—who was willing to share a little time listening.

And so I sat, and heard about the lovely young cousin who'd died in a bomber, and how the V1 and V2 rockets came over Mitcham and nearly made another hole in Aunt Bobbie's roof, and how part of what used to be over the way was reduced to rubble and the road was renamed and rerouted, and how Ben used to play in the ruins when he was small, because they took a long time to be cleared away after the war ended.

"Dear me," she said, after about ten minutes. "I've forgotten what it was you asked me."

"Did Ben write to you or ring you or come to see you after he sent that letter?" I asked.

"He didn't," Edith said. "I haven't heard from him at all since. Although it's not unusual. He's dreadful about staying in touch. I used to take him to task about it. But he'd always say he meant to, and he'd apologise. I once asked him what he was doing with all of his time. And he said he was thinking up stories."

"Stories...? Did he want to be a writer?"

"Perhaps," Edith mused. "Though he never wrote anything down. I remember when he was small he used to tell himself stories in bed. I once listened at his door and he was amusing himself with a tale about a boy who lived in a tree and didn't go to school. But he had to fight off magical dragons and he had a best friend who was a fairy. A boy fairy. With wings. And short trousers."

I laughed. That sounded just like the Ben I recalled from that Christmas with my toy castle and Sir Lancelot.

"Ben didn't involve you in any of his financial affairs, did he?" I asked.

"He pays for this flat," Edith said.

"Does he?"

"Oh yes. An amount is automatically withdrawn every month from his bank."

Damn, I thought. No human intervention required. I wondered about the legalities of having a word with Sophie's sister.

"You've been very helpful," I said, getting to my feet. "Thank you."

"You're welcome. Your father isn't alive, is he?"

"He isn't," I confirmed. "He died in 1995."

"Far too young," Edith said.

"He was," I agreed.

"Your mother must still be alive though."

"She is."

"Mandy Green. I must remember to send her a

little note."

"She'd like that. I'll have her send you one so you have her address."

I let myself out, and said goodbye to Maureen, and walked back to my car for a smoke.

#

I knew it was going to put Dom on the spot, and his girlfriend Sophie even more so. But the person who stood to get into the most trouble was Sophie's sister, Kris, the temp who was working at the bank.

Fortunately, it was her last week there, as the woman she'd been hired to replace was coming back from her leave. Even more fortunately, Kris knew her way around the bank's computer systems, and didn't seem particularly concerned that what I was asking her to do wasn't at all ethical, and was very likely against the law. I put it down to her previous employment with the imprisoned embezzler.

Kris waited until her last day to download and print Ben's account information, and then came round on the weekend to deliver it in person.

My flat's on the first floor of a Georgian-period conversion, my open plan kitchen and lounge created out of what used to be the main drawing room at the front of the house, my bedroom at the back constituting most of a second drawing room, and the former ante-room between the two now a very compact but functional loo.

Over green tea and take-out sushi, which Kris had

very kindly collected on her way from the tube station, she presented me with a five year history of Ben's financial transactions. Everything looked very ordinary. Royalty deposits for his music, direct debits for bills—including his mum's care home—credit card payments, cash taken from ATMs, cheques paid. He certainly wasn't lacking for money. Kris had even thought to include Ben's credit card statements.

"He's got other cards," she said. "This one doesn't show much usage at all, unfortunately."

She was right. Ben had kept it active by putting through the odd transaction every few months, but it obviously wasn't his primary way to pay. I could see transfers going out to at least two other credit card companies not attached to the bank. But unless I wanted to do something completely dodgy and also highly illegal, I wasn't going to get my hands on those details. I'm not that brave. And I didn't fancy sharing a cell with Kris's former boss.

As I looked over the printouts, I realized that everything had changed in the summer of 2013. Nearly all of his direct debits for things like electricity, gas, phone, home insurance and a monitored alarm system had come to a full stop. The one exception was the care home—the payments continued to be taken out, uninterrupted. There were no ATM withdrawals, no cheques written.

And Ben's royalties had continued to be paid in, the result being that his bank balance was now enviably healthy.

I knew Ben had a house near Hatfield in

Hertfordshire, a secluded cottage surrounded by trees and fields at the end of a narrow paved lane.

After Kris left, I did a search for the place online. I wasn't completely surprised to learn that he'd sold it and that it was currently up for sale again. What did surprise me was that the sale had taken place in 2012. Well before his disappearance. And yet he'd never changed the address on his bank statements.

"He opted for paperless delivery," Kris said, when I rang her to confirm what I'd discovered. "He only had to log into his account to see his statements."

And since Kris was no longer working there, I'd lost any chance I might have had to find out the last time Ben had checked in.

And where had he lived after he'd sold his house?

#

I looked online but I couldn't find any music festivals in 2013 featuring Ben Quigley. Or even mentioning him as being in the lineup.

I made a few more phone calls. I tried the other members of Figgis Green: the guy on bass—my uncle Mitch; the drummer—my dad's cousin Roland Black; the fiddler who was now producing records—Peter Chedwick. None of them had heard anything.

"Other than that woman who reckoned she was Ben's illegitimate daughter," Pete said.

"What woman?" I asked.

"Can't recall her name but I'm sure there something mentioned in the papers. Would have been six or seven years ago. I'm surprised you don't remember."

"Six or seven years ago I was at sea," I said. "I wasn't really on top of the news."

"I remember," Pete said, with understanding. "It was just after your Emma died in that fire, wasn't it?"

"It was," I confirmed.

"Anyway I don't expect it's all that important. She claimed she could prove he was her father but I seem to recall in the end they did a DNA test and there was no relationship. Have you tried his manager?"

"I didn't know he still had one."

"Probably in name only. Never taken off the books. Bob Rayling. Hang on and I'll get you his number."

"Pete's right," Bob Rayling said. "I used to handle his bookings but haven't done anything for him since…" He checked his computer. "2010."

I was sitting in a chair at an address very near to where The Blue Devil was. It was exactly the sort of Soho office you'd imagine, a black doorway in a nondescript wall, three flights of squeaky stairs—no lift—and a narrow hallway smelling of damp wood and even damper brick.

Bob Rayling seemed to be the sole proprietor, although there were two old wooden desks, and the second one showed signs of recent occupation: an empty paper cup from Starbucks, some notes on lined paper, three pens, and a couple of CDs. There was only one computer, however, and it was on Bob's desk. It looked old—it had a bulky tower and a monitor that was CRT-style, not a flat screen.

There were posters and photos on the walls that looked as though they'd been there for decades. Pop groups and performers you'd associate with big shoulders and big hair and glam lips and eyes. One or two names who'd managed to transcend the decades and stay relevant.

"Figgis," he said, leaning back in his chair, which was wooden and on wheels and had the capacity to swivel. "You related to Tony and Mandy?"

"My parents," I said.

"You in the business too?"

"I am," I said, and I told him about The Blue Devil.

"Nice," he said. "Jazz. Not my thing, unfortunately."

"You and my son," I said.

"I can't tell you much about Ben. Also unfortunately. The last time we spoke was 2010, as I said."

"Do you remember anything about a woman who claimed she was his illegitimate daughter?"

"He had a few of those," Bob chuckled. "Never came to anything."

"The most recent one," I said.

Bob raised a finger, as if to ask me to wait. He rode around in his chair, and, without standing up, consulted a drawer in a filing cabinet.

"Here we are." He presented me with two clippings from newspapers. "I saved them. Always save press that mention my clients."

I read over the stories. The same picture was in both. She did have a passing resemblance to Ben— her nose, and around her mouth. Her name was Susan Collingwood and she'd claimed that her mum had met Ben Quigley backstage after a Figgis Green concert in 1968 and had slept with him that night and had thereafter regularly informed her daughter, from the moment she'd been able to understand the words, that Ben Quigley was her natural father.

The second story was from about a year later, the newspaper trying to milk it for all its worth, even though the DNA test had proved to be negative. Susan was now heartbroken and suffering from depression. She'd truly believed Ben Quigley was her dad. But since her mum had now married for the 6th time and had gone to live in a small town in rural Mexico, she'd fallen out with her. The story was now about how she hoped to convince the public to crowd-fund her airfare to Mexico to mend the fences. As it were.

I gave the two clippings back to Bob.

"Do you know anything about a music festival about four years ago that Ben might have played at?"

Bob shook his head. "It wasn't arranged through me. 2010 was the last time. Told you."

"Thanks," I said. "I just thought you might have had other acts who were there. I'm trying to find a name."

Bob gave me a shrug, and I left.

#

I wasn't sure if Rick Redding would be helpful, considering the animosity between him and Ben and the circumstances surrounding Rick's departure from Figgis Green and Ben's subsequent arrival. But I'd met Rick on board the *Star Sapphire* when I was gigging at sea, so I thought I might as well ask.

"God love you, Jason," he said, over the phone. "How long's it been?"

"Five years," I told him.

"You still on the boats?"

"Gave it up after the *Sapphire* went down."

"Don't blame you, son. That sort of experience'll put the fear of God into anyone. I've not been on a boat since, though Carly's still keen. Wants to cruise the Med this winter. What's up?"

"Dom's filming a documentary about Ben Quigley and he's appointed me his chief researcher. I was wondering if you'd heard anything about him…met up with him at all…?"

"Not since we done that music festival in the middle of nowhere, when was it? 2013?"

I should have checked with him first.

"Where's the middle of nowhere?"

"Rural Canada, mate. Halfway to the North Pole. I was still managing Shag Pile. They were playing gigs all over western Canada so I went along on their bus. Quigley was one of the other headliners, solo act."

"Canada's a big country…"

"You're bloody telling me."

"Could you be a bit more specific about the location?"

"Somewhere north of Edmonton. That's all I know. What's that tune by Duane Eddy? *Forty Miles of Bad Road?* Try about three hundred."

"Did you speak to him?"

"Who, Quigley? Once or twice. We've never been mates."

"I understand," I said. "Did he seem OK to you?"

"Difficult to tell, son. Not knowing his usual state of mind."

"And he didn't say anything about what he was doing after the festival?"

"Not a word. He disappeared soon after that, though, didn't he?"

"What was the name of the festival?" I asked. "I've tried an online search. Nothing mentioning Ben."

"Disturbing the Peace," Rick said.

I laughed. "Very apt."

"It was a one-off thing. Middle of a farmer's field. I'm not surprised you couldn't find it."

"Can you remember the name of the nearest town?"

Rick had to think.

"Peace River," he said. "I think that must have been it."

"Makes sense," I said. "Where did you stay?"

"Can't remember, mate. Hotel number ten out of fifteen that summer."

"But Ben might have stayed there too…"

"He did. His room was down the hall from mine."

"Thanks," I said. "You've actually been really helpful."

"Great chatting with you again, mate. Come round for drinks. Carly'd love to see you again."

"I will," I promised, and rang off.

#

I tried a search for the music festival that had been called Disturbing the Peace, but came up empty. So I rang the local newspaper, the *Northern Rocket*, in Peace River and introduced myself and asked them. And a woman there named Alison McCall was able to find it in their archives. She emailed me the stories they'd done on it, and some advertising, and a couple of photos.

I asked if anyone specifically recalled interviewing Ben Quigley, or seeing him perform but again, nothing.

"How about the hotel where the acts stayed?" I tried.

"The 12 Foot Davis Inn," Alison said.

"You sound fairly sure of that."

"I am. I was still at university and I had a summer job there that year. I was working the overnight shift at the front desk."

"Would you remember Ben Quigley checking in or checking out?"

"Unfortunately not...I'd have been off-shift."

I took a chance. I asked her if she'd be able to find out when, exactly, Ben had left the hotel.

"Guest information's considered confidential," she reminded me.

"You and I both know that, Alison. But you're a reporter. If you were digging about researching a story...and you knew your way around that hotel's reservation system...what would you do?"

"Leave it with me," she said.

She rang me back later in the day.

"You didn't hear this from me," she said.

"I didn't," I agreed.

"Ben Quigley checked in on July 18th, 2013. He had the Jacuzzi Room. There's no record of him checking out."

"Sorry...?"

"There's a folio with check-in and check-out times, sundry expenses, that kind of stuff. He had a reservation for four nights. In on the 18th, the festival was on the weekend—the 20th and 21st— and he was supposed to check out on the morning of July 22nd. But he didn't. I guess the front desk assumed he'd decided to stay an extra day...I remember the hotel cleared out after the festival ended so it wasn't like they needed his room."

"Did housekeeping leave any notes on the folio?"

"It doesn't look like it."

"Just wondering if they'd have noticed whether

his clothes and bags and guitars were still there."

"There's nothing on the file. Anyway, on the morning of the 24th someone paid the bill in full—cash—and the front desk closed the file."

"It wasn't Ben who paid up?"

"Can't tell. There's just an entry showing six nights and sundries paid up in cash."

"Do you have a copy of the folio there?"

"Not that I can admit to…"

"Could you email it to me?"

"Of course not," Alison said, and, moments later, it appeared in my Inbox.

I looked over the entries.

I knew Ben had been in England the month before. The letter to his mum had a London postmark. He'd flown to Canada after that, and presumably had a return ticket.

As Alison had noted, hotel guest—and airline passenger—information was confidential. But it was my lucky day. Ben had made his hotel reservation through a travel agency—We Tour the World—it was right there on the folio. And if We Tour the World had made his hotel reservation, the chances were high that they'd also booked his flights.

It was time to give Katey a call.

#

I'd met Katey Shawcross aboard the *Sapphire* five years earlier. She was with a group of travel agents, and we'd fallen briefly and astoundingly in love.

We'd probably have stayed together if I hadn't been so keen to see what was on the other side of the Pacific. Katey wasn't interested. She hated the business. I left her in London and when I came back two years later I discovered she hadn't abandoned the travel industry after all—she'd just found another way to make a living from it. She was working for an agency that specialized in corporate accounts, business only, no more having to deal with tropical honeymoons battered by hurricanes and beachfront hotels turning out to be a hundred feet down a rocky cliff with rickety steps and no access for wheelchairs.

I invited her to lunch at Rules. It's my favourite restaurant, with a fabulous history (established in 1798, with a menu that features traditional English food—the game comes with a warning that it may contain lead shot!). They know me there, as it's located in Maiden Lane, close to Covent Garden and a ten minute walk from The Blue Devil.

"I haven't eaten here in years," she said, sipping one of their house cocktails, Kate Middleton's "Royal 29"—No. 3 Gin, Finlandia Vodka, Lillet & Crystallised Violet Petals. "In fact, I think the last time was probably with you."

I'd stopped smoking after Emma died and I'd stopped drinking as well. The decision not to drink had stuck. I was having a posh fizzy water.

"I think it was too," I said.

Katey had ordered the Fillet of Salmon, and I'd ordered Wild Boar Pie. Normally I'd have had their

Steak and Kidney Pie. But our waiter had suggested a change, and I'd caught the look of abject horror on Katey's face at the mention of wild boar, so I took him up on the offer.

"You did that just to annoy me, didn't you?" she said.

"I did," I admitted.

"What can I help you with?" she asked, good-naturedly.

I'd mentioned, when I'd rung her, that I might possibly require her assistance.

"Do you know anyone who works at We Tour the World?"

"I don't think so. I've heard of them, though—they arrange trips for pop groups. Why?"

I told her.

"You're right about client confidentiality. I doubt they'd give me any information about Ben Quigley's travel arrangements even if I was best friends with their managing director."

"Suppose you were to ring them up and tell them you were Ben's sister and you were trying to retrace his last steps before he disappeared."

Katey gave me a look.

"Suppose you were to ring them up and tell them you were hired by Ben's family to audit his accounts and you needed to have all the details of the last trip he booked through them," she suggested, instead.

"I love you, Katey."

"I know," she said. "But you'll never get me back into bed with you if you insist on eating wild boar."

#

We Tour the World's office was in Fitzrovia, north of Oxford Street, midway between Tottenham Court Road and Oxford Circus tube stations. It was on the ground floor of a red brick building that had three storeys of private flats above it, with quite a nice-looking pub on the corner.

I was well-prepared for my appointment with Lesley, the senior travel agent who'd handled Ben's itinerary. I'd got some business cards printed from an online place and had them shipped Express so that they arrived within two days. I was now Robert Kingston, BSc Hons (Applied Accounting), MBA and ACCA, and I hoped like hell Lesley wasn't going to do any followup checks on my legitimacy. The phone number I'd listed was real—it was my mobile—and it was my address as well—just in case.

I'd dressed the part: a dark grey wool suit that I'd got from John Lewis. And a pale blue shirt and a navy and dark blue Grenadine tie. Black brogues and black socks and for the finishing touch, I'd added a black leather briefcase.

I'm not sure where I found the bravado. I reasoned that I wasn't impersonating Ben, I was impersonating an accountant. And travel records weren't in the same league as financial statements. I wasn't sure if what I was doing was illegal but I was fairly certain I was compromising some ethics. I didn't care.

I arrived five minutes early for my appointment. Lesley was available and took me into an office that wasn't hers, and shut the door, then sat down at the desk and invited me to do the same.

"Here we are," she said, calling up Ben's file on the agency's computer. She also had a physical folder, bright orange, which she opened. "Paper backup," she said. "Never put your faith in technology."

I slid her my business card and repeated the story I'd told her over the phone, that I'd been hired by Ben's mum to track down his last travel arrangements, as nobody had seen or heard from him since 2013.

"Shame about that," Lesley said. "He seemed rather a lovely man. Getting on a bit—but he had a brilliant sense of humour. He was quite adamant that he wanted to do that music festival. None of us had ever heard of it but it seemed to be quite well organized. Quite a challenge to get to."

I went around to her side of the desk to look at the computer screen.

"Air Canada to Calgary and then a connecting flight on to Grande Prairie. Peace River's got an airport but it's serviced by an airline with a fleet of Beechcrafts and Ben wasn't very keen on small planes."

"I don't blame him," I said. "I'm the same."

"So he flew into Grande Prairie, which is two hours away by car, and he drove the rest of the way himself. I was a bit worried because of his age but he said he'd be fine, so I arranged a compact car, and booked him into the 12 Foot Davis Inn—" She looked at me. "Intriguing name for a hotel—I wonder where it came from." She went back to the reservation details. "He took two guitars with him as well as his regular luggage…and he requested a window seat at the left rear of each plane."

She printed off the itinerary and the booking and ticketing details and all of the invoices.

"There you are," she said.

I read over the pages. Ben's address and telephone number were on the invoices. It was the same address as the one on his bank statements— the house that he'd sold the year before.

"His car was returned three days late," I said.

"Interesting," Lesley said. "Yes. And not by him. There's someone else's signature on the agreement. And that person paid cash for the entire rental. They sent us a copy because we always take care of the payments for our clients. In this case, it looks like we didn't have to."

"Would that be the same for his hotel?"

Lesley checked the folder.

"You're right," she said. "He stayed for two extra nights…and the entire reservation was paid for in cash. It must have been while I was on hols and one of the other agents looked after processing all of this…"

"Can you tell whether Ben used the return part of his plane ticket?" I asked.

Lesley leafed through the pages, a slight frown on

her face.

"His fare was 100% non-ref...he wouldn't have got a refund except perhaps a small amount of tax...but look, yes...someone cancelled his flights coming home...and he didn't rebook."

Somewhere in the midst of all of the airport designators and flight times and strings of mysterious code known only to travel agents and airline employees was the confirmation I'd been looking for. Ben Quigley had never left Canada.

"I suppose he could have come home at a later date," Lesley said, "and paid for it himself, without going through us. If you were to involve the police, for instance, I'm sure they'd be able to find out."

"Thanks," I said, collecting all of the papers and popping them into my briefcase. "I'll ask Mrs. Quigley if she wishes to do that."

"And if we can be of any further help..."

"Yes, of course. I'll be in touch."

I'd never impersonated anyone before. And as I left the travel agency and walked back towards the tube at Tottenham Court Road, I was filled with an odd kind of excitement. I'd pulled it off. I'd pretended to be someone who I was not and I'd played the part perfectly. And I'd got the information I needed.

#

I had a week's break coming up at The Blue Devil.

"I'm going to Canada," I said, to Dom. "Do you want to come with me?"

I was planning to take the same flights as Ben, but without the restrictive conditions. I'd have loved to have booked Business Class, with its embarrassment of amenities and room to stretch out, but the cost would have been prohibitive. Premium Economy would do.

I have money. Dad left a sizeable amount to all of us—mum, Angie and me—when he died, plus there was a life insurance policy which paid out well to mum, and she shared it with us. And then there's all the continuing royalties from his music—not just with Figgis Green, but his other projects too, things he wrote, produced, arranged... I'm actually in the same boat as that bloke Hugh Grant played in *About a Boy*...but without the annoying Christmas song. I don't need to work...but I want to.

And music's not work anyway. It's what I do. It's sustenance.

"Can't dad," Dom said, reminding me. "University."

"Ah," I said. "Of course."

"Is Ben Quigley in Canada, then?"

"I'm not sure. I'm going to find out."

I'd looked up Peace River on Google Maps. It really was in the middle of nowhere—a satellite view plonked it down on a patchwork of green and grey squares, on Highway 2, on the banks of the immense river which gave the town its name. It had a population of 6,800, a museum, a ballpark and a giant wooden statue of 12 Foot Davis…aka Henry Fuller Davis, an American fur trader who staked a twelve foot land claim during the Cariboo gold rush and made enough money to open a trading post close to the town of Peace River. The twelve foot wooden statue was on a hilltop overlooking the town, along with his grave.

Absurdly pleased with myself for having discovered the origin of the name of Ben's hotel, I booked myself into the same room Ben had—a king sized bed, a microwave and a fridge, and a Jacuzzi (the only one in the hotel, apparently). The idea of having a Jacuzzi tucked into the corner of the room fascinated me. The photo gallery sold me. And it would make up for not having a pillow, a duvet, a toiletry kit and a private pod on the plane.

I also made arrangements to pick up a car at Grande Prairie airport. I had no idea what the road from Grande Prairie to Peace River was going to be like in the dead of winter. Google Earth didn't offer much in the way of clues—only a long swath of straight highway cutting across the countryside that would take me two hours to navigate.

It was going to be an eight-and-a-half-hour flight from London on a 787, with a three-hour layover in Calgary, and then another ninety minutes on a Dash-8 to Grande Prairie, topped off by a 200 km drive to Peace River. With all of that in mind, I allowed myself the luxury of a taxi to Heathrow.

PART TWO

I have never, in my entire life, been so fundamentally freezing fucking cold.

I should have known what to expect when I looked out of the window of the plane and saw everything below completely covered in snow. I should have listened—really listened—when the Captain came over the PA to inform us we'd shortly be landing in Calgary, the local time was 2.55pm and the temperature on the ground was a balmy -26°C with a low that night expected to be in the vicinity of -30°C.

But it didn't really sink in.

It's one of those things you seriously cannot understand until you've actually experienced it.

I had a three hour layover in Calgary before my flight to Grande Prairie. I got myself through the CBSA Primary Inspection and Customs, and lugged my suitcase off the carousel, and my next order of business was to find the airport's smoking area.

It was outside.

I was wearing a short padded winter jacket and lined hiking boots that looked and felt more like trainers. I had a pair of leather gloves stuffed into my pockets. I zipped up the jacket and put the gloves on and stepped through the airport doors.

I once had an uncle who worked for British Airways. He loved Canada. He flew there as often as he could for his holidays. He particularly loved the Canadian prairies in the winter. From Uncle Fred I learned that the winter weather in Canada was "exhilarantly bracing."

Those are not the words I would have used to describe the moment Calgary's -26°C winter chill met my woefully unprepared face, hands, feet and body. It was penetrating, aggressive and relentlessly unmerciful. I couldn't see myself lasting two minutes outside, let alone the time it would take to smoke one cigarette.

I turned around and went back into the terminal and vowed, first, that my Uncle Fred was insane, and second, that I would give up my evil habit there and then.

Over the next couple of hours I chewed my way through three packages of gum and managed to distract myself with a Bento box and massive amounts of hot green tea at a Japanese restaurant on the Mezzanine level of Canadian Departures.

And then, after committing a further indignity to my unwinterized body by forcing it to walk across the tarmac to board a tiny, prop-driven Dash-8, I was on my way, at last, to Grande Prairie.

#

Ben had done this journey in the summer.

In the summer, Grande Prairie—and Peace River—would have stayed light until quite late in the evening.

In the winter, this far north, the sun gave up early. and it was dark by the time we landed at the little airport and I braced myself, one more time, for the ball-shrinking icewalk from the plane to the terminal.

I don't think the guy at the car rental booth saw a lot of Brits come through at that time of the year. He seemed quite amused by my accent—then again, it might have been my completely inadequate jacket and useless leather gloves. I'd arranged for a decent midsize car and, as I was signing the forms and agreeing to every kind of insurance on offer, I had a clever thought, and asked about the possibility of snow tires.

"Our cars come with all weather tires," the guy said "They're good as long as you don't brake suddenly in the snow or hit glare ice. Where you going?"

I told him, and he obligingly gave me a road report that included words like "mostly clear" and "some slippery sections" and "caution in low lying areas and on hills".

"So you're ok driving in Canadian winter conditions?" he checked.

"Absolutely," I lied.

He gave me the keys, and my contract, and reminded me that their cars all had a No Smoking policy and that if they found any trace at all of cigarettes, including the merest whiff of burnt tobacco, I'd be landed with a hefty cleaning bill. He told me where to find the car, and then added: "Don't forget to unplug it."

I had not rented an electric car. And I wasn't absolutely certain what he meant, until I'd trudged out through the snow, dragging my suitcase behind me like a defective sled, and located my vehicle, and discovered that it was, indeed, plugged into an outlet in the fence that ran along the front of the stalls.

And then I recalled my insane Uncle Fred, and his wondrous tales of engine bloc heaters that kept oil and batteries from freezing in parked cars when the temperatures fell below zero.

My car came with a handy heavy-duty bright orange extension cord, which I disconnected and stowed in the back with my luggage. I sat with the engine running and the interior heat blowing full blast for about ten minutes, trying to warm myself up. And then, I set the GPS on my phone to navigate me out of the little city and out onto Highway 2.

#

It was about eight o'clock by the time the lights of Grande Prairie disappeared behind me. And my body and brain were reminding me that it was 3am in London. Three o'clock in the morning's normal for me. But I don't usually get up until noon. And I'd had an extremely early start and a very long journey and travelling knocks the wind out of you. I cursed myself for not letting Katey make my travel arrangements—she'd have sensibly suggested spending the night in Grande Prairie and setting out for Peace River the next day.

It was a very long and a very dark drive on the wrong side of the road. The car had Bluetooth so on my way out of Grande Prairie I synch'd the music on my phone and had Ben Quigley's Strat—and Figgis Green—to keep me company for the first part of the drive, and then Herbie Hancock and Charlie Mingus for the next bit. Other than the occasional truck coming at me in the opposite direction, and a few cars that were spaced out at intervals ahead of me, their rear lights shining red in the blackness, I was on my own. Occasionally the road, for no apparent reason, angled off to the north, and then back to the east, and even less occasionally, I had to slow down to pass through a settlement of people... Sexsmith...Rycroft...there was an interesting two-lane suspension bridge at a place called Dunvegan— I saw it lit up by the high beams of my headlamps— and then a long slow climb out of the valley towards a town called Fairview, which marked the halfway point of the trip.

I was in the process of congratulating myself that I hadn't encountered any ice or snow along the way when, all of a sudden, and with no warning whatsoever, the car began to slide. I was going about 100kph, the speed limit. I had microseconds to react and it took everything I had not to panic, not to hit the brakes, to remember Uncle Fred's wisely-learned instructions for ice-driving: turn your wheels into the skid.

I did, and the car gracefully completed a 360° turn in the middle of the highway and, after avoiding a spin-off into a snow-filled ditch, came to a complete stop on the other side of the road, facing the oncoming traffic.

I sat for a few seconds, listening to my heart pounding and trying to get my breathing back to normal. Then I realized there were bright white lights roaring towards me and I slid the car back to the other lane three seconds ahead of a huge big-rig truck that likely would have flattened me if I'd waited any longer.

I was in no shape to drive on. I needed a smoke. And a pee. Very badly. I didn't dare stop the engine. I rolled the driver's side window down about four inches and literally caught my breath as the freezing night air hit my face. I lit up and blew the smoke out through the gap, then opened the door a crack and tossed the finished cigarette into the snow and extinguished it as I relieved myself.

As I closed the window I caught sight of something I'd only ever seen in pictures and heard about from others: a magnificent burst of Northern Lights—a glimmering dance of luminescent green that made me think of the peaks and dips on a graphic audio display, with much-softened edges.

They stayed with me for the next 100 km, all the way into Peace River, and then, inexplicably, faded away into the starlit night as I drove into the parking lot of the 12 Foot Davis Hotel.

The night clerk was friendly and efficient.

"You remembered to plug your car in, right?" she checked, as she handed me my keycard.

I had not. I went back outside and retrieved the thick orange extension cord and connected it to the plug hanging out of the car's front grillwork, and then shoved the other end into the outlet.

"Gonna be a cold one tonight," the clerk said, helpfully, after I'd run back inside, cursing my flimsy English jacket.

"Minus thirty in Calgary," I offered.

"Minus twenty-three in the valley."

"Almost a heatwave," I agreed.

My room was exactly as it had been pictured—with the famous Jacuzzi occupying the corner, along with some fluffy white towels and a laminated instruction card. I imagined some randy trucker, fresh from a long haul even further north than this, stepping in for a soak with a preferred lady visitor, then repairing to the king sized bed with two tins of beer and a porn film on the TV.

I undressed, skipped the soak and the porn, and collapsed into bed without bothering to unpack.

And when I eventually woke up, it was past eleven

in the morning. I'd missed the complementary hot breakfast, and I wanted to know where Ben Quigley had gone after vacating this room.

#

The Jacuzzi room was Non-Smoking.

It was my own fault; I hadn't thought to ask when I was making my reservation. I'd made assumptions and now I was desperate for a cigarette, there were no ashtrays, a little cardboard stand-up sign on the table was reminding me why, and the window, which I could easily have slid open in warmer weather, was frozen shut under a thick layer of ice.

I lit my cigarette in the loo, switching on the fan and blowing the smoke down the drain in the sink— a trick I'd learned from fellow crewmembers aboard the *Star Sapphire*, who occupied cabins where lighting up was strictly prohibited.

I pulled my favourite battered Levi's and a plain navy blue t-shirt from Next out of my case, laced up my hiking shoes and collected my jacket out of the cupboard by the door. And then, foolishly, in the hotel's lobby, I checked the temperature on my phone.

It was -13°C, which wasn't nearly as low as the night before, but still cold enough for the windows of my car to be covered in a hard frost. I unplugged the extension cord and stowed it, and started the engine, and while the heater blew hot air onto the windscreen, I looked in the boot for something I could use on the rest of the windows. I found a long wooden stick with a brush on one end and a plastic scraper on the other. By the time I'd made the windows presentable I'd worked up enough sweat to make me forget my wholly inadequate winter clothing.

I threw the scraper in the back, and drove down the hill and across the bridge into town.

The Riverfront Cafe wasn't really on the river—which was frozen solid and covered in snow—and didn't even have a view of it. But it was in a part of the town called Riverfront, and it seemed to be the most popular restaurant in the area for lunch.

Alison McCall was waiting for me at a table beside a window. She had long straight brown hair and was wearing a bright red headband and a red t-shirt and jeans and her fur-hooded parka was slung over the back of her chair. I'd say she was in her mid-twenties.

"Jason!" she said, with a wave.

I unzipped my jacket.

"Did you check me out online?" I inquired humorously, wondering fleetingly how she'd recognized me.

"You look English," she said.

I sat down, throwing my jacket onto an empty chair.

"And that," she added. "Definitely not something any self-respecting Canadian would ever wear in February."

"I need to buy one of those," I said, nodding at her parka.

"I'll take you shopping after lunch," she promised.

I glanced over the menu, which offered a three-egg breakfast all day long, prepared in multiple ways. I was definitely in the mood for an omelette with bacon, cheese, ham and sausage and an order of hash browns on the side.

"So, what else have you found out about Ben Quigley?" Alison asked.

I brought her up to date.

"So you think he never left Peace River?"

"That's what I think."

"This is a really small place, Jason. Even the people who live out of town—everyone who has an acreage or a farm—they all come into Peace River to get their groceries, to gas up and go to church—everyone knows everybody else. They'd notice someone like Ben. The same way I noticed you."

"English accent a dead giveaway."

"It's very attractive," she said.

"I like American accents," I said. Alison gave me a look. "Canadian," I said quickly, correcting myself.

"If he was still here I think we'd have known. On top of everything else, Ben Quigley's famous. To people your age, anyway. I have to admit I had to look him up when he played the festival. I'd never heard of him before. But if someone like that was living in the area, we'd all be talking about it. You'd never be able to keep something like that a secret."

"What if he didn't want to be found?"

Alison shrugged. "I guess he could have got himself a place out in the country. He'd still need to eat, though. And get gas for his car."

Our food arrived. My omelette was immense, its size unheard of in London. "Someone else could be doing that for him," I said. "Someone else paid for his hotel room and returned his car to the rental agency."

"I guess so." Alison tucked into her quesadilla. "Where would you even start looking for him, then?"

"I thought I might have a chat with whoever organized the music festival. Have a look at Ben's contract, maybe find some clues there..."

"Good luck with that. The promoter's long gone. The festival was a disaster. Very little advance PR, security was a mess, catering was a joke, it rained, bills weren't paid...he took off with whatever money was collected, the paperwork, everything. The RCMP have a warrant out for his arrest."

"Would I have heard of him?"

"Jeremy Bowden."

"Doesn't ring a bell."

"Total scam artist. It's probably not even his real name. Extremely charming. English. And a serial womanizer."

I gave Alison a look.

"Not me," she said. "I'm too wise to fall for that kind of shit. Brenda Hubenko. I went to school with her. She cuts hair at Styles 'n' Smiles."

I put Brenda's name into my phone, and the name of the hair salon. I didn't think chatting with her would be all that helpful, but you never knew.

Alison turned around in her seat, because there was a commotion at the cash register, near the door. Two women were shouting at one another. One was still inside the restaurant, the other on her way out to the parking lot.

The woman who was still inside the restaurant seemed about my age. She had long wavy blonde hair tied back into a ponytail fastened with a large pink silk hibiscus. She was wearing an unzipped winter coat, and a checked shirt and jeans and lace-up workboots, and the main point of her shouting appeared to be to accuse the other woman of punching a hole in one of her outbuildings and stealing a supply of moose and deer hides which had been stored there

"My yard's a mess!" she screamed, through the restaurant's doorway, which she was now holding open, sending a blast of frigid air through to where Alison and I were sitting.

"I've never been anywhere near your yard!" the other woman shouted back. "Maybe you should check the trees! Maybe you should check for bears!"

"The bears are all hibernating! And the last one who came near the house last summer got a couple of shotgun shells in the ass!"

"Yeah well maybe he'll wake up and come back with his friends and take out your ass and then we can all get some peace and quiet around here!"

The woman who was outside got into her car and skidded away in the snow. The blonde woman with the pink hibiscus came back to the cash register to pay for her lunch.

Around us, the other customers seemed amused, but unconcerned.

"Miriam," Alison said. "She lives on an old farm about 30k north of here. She makes mukluks and moccasins and sells them in town and at local fairs. She's off her meds again."

"Does this happen often?"

"A couple of times a year," Alison shrugged. "She's been banned from most places for shoplifting. She has to drive to Grimshaw for her groceries. And she shows up regularly at the hospital claiming to be in serious pain. She's fond of fibromyalgia."

Alison caught my questioning look.

"My best friend's a doctor," she said. "On call at Emergency."

She was finishing up her quesadilla.

"And her house is haunted."

"Your best friend's?"

"Miriam's," Alison said. "She lived there with her parents and then they were killed in a car accident and she hired some workmen to come in and renovate the place but they refused to show up after a couple of weeks because they claimed it was possessed. They had a lot of weird feelings and heard a lot of strange noises. And people have claimed when Miriam's not home they can see lights in the house mysteriously turning themselves on and off."

"Doesn't seem to keep the bears away," I said, humorously.

"I don't believe in ghosts," Alison said. "I think it's just Miriam, telling stories."

"How do you explain the lights?"

"Automatic timers?" she said, and I realized how thick I sounded.

Miriam, meanwhile, had finished paying for her lunch and left the restaurant. Moments later I saw— and heard—her driving past the window in a dirty farm truck that had a cracked windscreen and was covered in dents and rust.

"Grocery run to Grimshaw," Alison said.

I was nearly finished my omelette. Scraping frost off car windows in winter really brings on an appetite.

"Can we buy some proper boots as well?" I said.

#

I followed Alison over to Mukluks and More, a few blocks away from the restaurant, on 100th Street. She was driving a big Ford Explorer with tires that had thick deep treads which were much better adapted to winter in Peace River than the tires on the car I'd rented.

The roads had been cleared, the snow graded up on each side in uneven banks, but there was still a layer of hard packed ice on the pavement that required a degree of driving skill I wasn't sure I had.

I crawled along behind her Explorer, hoping I wouldn't have to stop suddenly, praying that distracted pedestrians would have more sense than to go out walking on such a cold day.

Mukluks and More was a little handicraft shop crammed with things people had made: hand-dipped candles and knitted scarves, soaps and essential oils, mittens and socks and caps, Christmas ornaments (on sale, prices slashed), jewellery and carvings and, of course, mukluks.

"This is where Miriam sells her stuff," I guessed, reading a little tag attached to a pair of fur-covered boots: Mukluks by Miriam. $150

"I prefer the real thing," Alison said. She directed me to a corner of the shop which featured work by members of the region's First Nations. The mukluks there were superior by far. A pair of hand-tanned moose hide boots caught my eye, finished with white rabbit fur and soft hide laces with pom-poms and beaded red flowers. $600.

I tried them on.

"You'd want to keep those for a special occasion," Alison advised. "They're good in deep dry snow, but useless when it gets slushy. And you'd need to wear about four layers of socks to keep your feet warm."

"I'll take them," I said to the sales clerk, who placed them on the counter.

"We'll go up the hill after this and get you into

some decent winter boots," Alison said. "Scarf and toque?"

She held up a six-foot long hand-knitted striped scarf in green and purple and bronze and grey, and a matching cap with a bobble on top.

"And of course, mitts."

They were made out of tan-coloured sheepskin. I carried everything up to the clerk and paid for it with my Amex.

"Need a bag?" the clerk checked.

"I'll wear them," I replied.

Over the bridge and up the hill, very near to where I was staying, a big box store that specialized in practical winter gear provided me with a pair of stylish-looking lace-up boots with buffalo leather uppers and insulated insides and soles that looked like they could equal Alison's snow tires when it came to traction.

And down the aisle we found a proper arctic down-filled parka, with a fur-lined hood and a storm flap and an activity rating of -40°C.

My new winter wardrobe was completed by three pairs of heavy duty thermal socks.

"Need a bag?" the clerk asked at the checkout.

"He'll wear them," Alison replied.

It was only about three in the afternoon by the time we'd finished, but the seven hour time change was beating me up again, and I was starting to fade.

I thanked Alison and promised to be in touch

later, possibly for another lunch, depending on the outcome of my investigations, and then I drove back to my hotel, plugged in the car, and trudged through the snow to the lobby.

I rang Dom from my room, hoping to update him with what I'd learned and also to share my delight at finally being warm and not on the constant verge of hypothermia, but his phone went to messaging. I left him a short, detailed explanation, then picked up the laminated instructions for the Jacuzzi. A twenty minute soak in a roomy tub filled with bubbling hot water seemed just the cure I needed for my jet lag.

I dropped a towel on the floor and dragged a chair over from the desk and put two more fluffy white towels on that, then pulled off all my clothes and stuck my hand in the water to test the temperature.

A jolt shot up my arm. It slammed into my chest, throwing me backwards. I crashed into the chair and rolled off it, onto the floor, writhing in pain. Paralyzed, unable to move, I gasped for air, focussing on the fire sprinkler in the ceiling, fighting to stay conscious.

The pain ripped through my entire body but thank God my feet were clear of the walls of the Jacuzzi. My hand was numb, my arm under attack by a thousand pins and needles, but I was alive. And after a few moments, I could move again.

I rolled as far away from the tub as I could. I sat up, then crawled onto the bed and stayed there for ten minutes, fifteen, trying to make sense of what had just happened.

I knew a guy who electrocuted himself in his studio. Something wasn't grounded properly. He picked up his guitar and plugged it in and died. I always thought it a particularly gruesome way to go, and wondered how long he'd been alive before his body had given up and his mind had gone dark. I wondered if he knew what had happened, and if he'd stayed conscious the entire time, or if he'd blacked out instantly, and had been spared the awareness that his heart had stopped and it would never beat again.

If I'd stepped into the tub instead of just popping my hand in, I might not have survived. The shock would have gone up my leg and I'd have tumbled over, and if total immersion in the charged water hadn't killed me, I would have drowned.

I picked up the phone and dialled the front desk and told them what had happened. Five minutes later someone was banging on my door.

I crawled off the bed, and pulled on my jeans, and staggered across the room to let them in.

#

"They've given me another room. Without a Jacuzzi."

I'd put all my clothes on again, and my new winter gear, and walked across the parking lot to a big barn of a restaurant that specialized in ten-page menus, very large cocktails and every cut of steak imaginable.

I'd rung Alison and she'd driven over immediately. It was still too early for dinner, but I honestly wasn't hungry. I just needed to be with someone.

"Are you ok? Do you want to see a doctor?"

"I'm ok," I said.

"I can call Karen at Emergency," Alison said, doubtfully.

"Everything's working and nothing's numb," I said. "And nothing hurts anymore. Much."

"Here's the number for the Health Centre anyway," she said, writing it down on a paper napkin and pushing it over to my side of the table. "They're open twenty-four hours."

The waitress brought our drinks and a plate of stuffed potato skins. Alison was having a spicy Caesar. I'd opted for a mug of very strong coffee.

"I'm surprised you're not shooting down straight whiskeys."

"I don't drink," I said.

"Ah," said Alison. "Understood. AA?"

"Personal choice. It got me into a lot of trouble."

"You must be a very strong person."

"My off-switch wasn't broken," I said, recalling conversations I'd had with friends who were dedicated to the Twelve Steps. "That's the only difference."

"Do they know what caused the short circuit in your Jacuzzi?" Alison asked.

I shook my head. "They've got an electrician looking into it."

"You could be my lead story in tomorrow's paper…"

"I'd rather not be," I said. "I grew up with journos and snappers chasing scoops. My parents got very good at protecting our privacy. I like the attention…but only when it's on my terms."

"Well, your hands have stopped shaking, anyway. You could probably take the hotel to court if it turns out to be their fault. In which case you should get checked out by a doctor so you have a medical report for your lawyer."

"*If* it turns out to be their fault," I said.

"It's certainly not yours."

"That's not what I was thinking."

Alison sipped her Caesar. "What were you thinking?"

"I wonder if it's possible somebody doesn't want me to find Ben?"

"That's a bit far-fetched."

"You're right," I said. "It is. Forget I mentioned it."

"And who would know anyway? You only just got here."

I had to agree with her. My rattled brain was wandering into odd corners.

"You said everyone here knows everyone else. Would the desk clerk who handled the cash for Ben's room have recognized the person who paid it?"

"I could ask her. She still works there. Sonia Melenchuck. I w—"

"You went to school with her," I guessed.

"I did," Alison smiled. "I'll give her a call. Anyway, if somebody did tamper with the wiring in your Jacuzzi they couldn't have just walked in and done it. They'd have to get access to your room. And know exactly what they were doing. If I say I'm doing a story, I might be able to find out what happened."

"OK," I said.

"I don't have to actually write the piece," she added, noting my hesitation.

"Thank you."

It was dark by the time I made my way back to the hotel. The booth behind ours had been taken over by a collection of heavily-bearded men in sleeveless khaki jackets and jeans held up with braces. They were drinking beer and complaining in loud Texas accents that they hadn't realized big game hunting season was over up here and they were damned if they were drivin' all the way back down to San Antonio without some trophies.

I saw their convoy in the parking lot: a posse of white half-ton trucks, one of them pulling a large covered trailer emblazoned with paintings of elk, moose and bears, each captioned with lines of scripture. Good ol' boys huntin' for Jesus. I sent up a prayer for the protection of Peace River's wildlife, and went to my new room on the second floor, where I was allowed to smoke.

I finished one cigarette, and then another, and then put my phone on Airplane Mode, and fell into bed.

#

I woke up to two messages.

The first was from Dom, acknowledging my successful shopping trip and suggesting that Ben might have had dark reasons for wanting to disappear.

"Inland revenue," said the text. "Or bad debts to bad people."

It might have been the first, but it definitely wasn't the second. Ben's bank accounts were solid. A third possibility was that he'd finally had enough, and, like Gerry Rafferty and Greta Garbo, he just wanted to be left alone.

And I'd have accepted that. I honestly would have understood that Ben didn't want to be found. I'd have passed the Jacuzzi incident off as a nasty accident, packed my bags and caught the next flight home and left him in peace. But for the next message.

It was from my mum, telling me that Ben's mum, Edith, had been taken into hospital and wasn't expected to live. The care home was trying to locate Ben to advise him. They'd contacted my mum because of Ben's connection to Figgis Green, and could I help? Edith was distressed and asking for her son.

Even if Ben had abandoned his life in England, he'd made sure his mum was taken care of before he left. And if it was me, even if I was sleeping on rocks in a cave and eating wild locusts for breakfast, I'd have appreciated being told that my mum was dying.

I needed to think.

Often, when I require solitude in order to sort through a dilemma or reason out an issue, I go for a drive in the country. Back home I'd have coaxed my old Volvo out of the side road near my flat and driven it north into the bedroom communities of the well-off, and puttered around leafy lanes listening to Dave Brubeck or John Coltrane while I made up my mind.

The countryside here didn't offer much by way of contemplative reflection, unless I wanted to pull off to the side of the road and ponder the endless white flatness of the snow-covered fields topped by an infinite canopy of icy blue sky.

The valley where the town was nestled seemed far more inviting.

I drove down the hill and across the bridge, and turned off the highway and backtracked through the edge of downtown until I found a built-up embankment running alongside the river, with a road beside it. Then I aimed the car north, meandering through a residential neighbourhood, Sonny Stitt's *Blue Devil Blues* on the Bluetooth, my brain working overtime to try and think of all the ways to try and find Ben.

I was about to concede that I'd be better off just hiring a private detective and paying for the expertise that I obviously didn't have, when I found myself at the town's cemetery.

I'd driven up a hill, past a rather nice little collection of big, newish houses. I hadn't expected the road to end where it did.

I stopped the car, and got out, and wandered through the gate. It was very quiet—as cemeteries often are—and the view was amazing: the wide frozen Peace River below, the western side of the valley beyond with its sage-coloured hills dusted with white, and in the cemetery, neat rows of polished granite memorials with unfamiliar names and tributes poking up out of a gently sloping snowfield.

And then, I stopped.

Something had guided me here, because I'd most definitely not consciously sought it out.

I was standing in front of a fairly new grave, its memorial stone shiny white, a metal vase at its base filled with faded plastic flowers. The name carved into the face of the memorial was Susan Frances Collingwood.

It was the same name as the woman who had claimed that Ben was her dad.

Couldn't be, I thought. How many Susan Collingwood's were there in the world?

I took a photo of the grave with my phone and then trudged back to my car, started the engine to warm up the interior, and did a search for old newspaper stories to see if I could find the ones that

Bob had shown me in his office. I had to join a British newspaper archive site that cost me £13 for a month's unlimited access, but I found them. Ben's Susan Collingwood was born in 1968 or 1969, after a one-night stand in Newcastle.

Peace River's Susan Collingwood was born on December 14th, 1968. And she'd died on July 23, 2013. Two days after Ben had been booked to perform at the music festival.

#

Ten minutes later I was back in my hotel room, studying the printout that showed Ben's car's rental return on July 25, three days late. The signature was impossible to make out but it couldn't have been Susan's anyway because she was dead by then.

I found her obituary, doing another online search with my phone.

Mrs. Susan Frances Collingwood. Born on December 14, 1968 in Newcastle, England. Passed away at the age of 44 years in Peace River, Alberta. Pre-deceased by her parents, Samuel Bailey and Florence Hernandez and by her husband Hector Collingwood. Survived by her sister Marian Bailey as well as a large circle of relatives and friends. Funeral arrangements etc.

I rang Alison.

"I was going to call you," she said. "I checked with Sonia and she says the cash to pay for Ben's room was delivered anonymously, in a sealed envelope, with a note. It was left at the desk."

"Nobody saw who dropped it off?"

"I guess not."

"No CCTV or security cameras?"

"The hotel doesn't have them," said Alison. "I also asked Sonia about your Jacuzzi and she says the electricians haven't said anything to her about what they found. I'll dig around some more and ask some more question. I know one of the electrical guys."

"You went to school with him." I guessed.

"Actually I didn't. But he's Karen's brother."

I told her what I'd found at the cemetery. And how Susan Collingwood was connected to Ben Quigley. I read her the obituary.

There was silence on the other end of the line. And then: "Wow."

"Do you remember her?"

"I do," Alison confirmed. "She worked at Styles 'n' Smiles with Brenda."

"Do you remember anything else about her?"

"I think she moved here…five or six years ago. I remember her accent—it attracted a lot of attention. It wasn't like yours."

"Susan was a Geordie," I said. "From the north of England. Where did she live?"

"I think she rented an apartment downtown."

"Do you know why she decided to move to Peace River?"

"She really kept to herself. I don't think she ever said."

"Odd," I said. "Hairdressers' chairs are usually

hotspots of gossip and intrigue." I paused. "Do you remember how she died? It's not mentioned in the obituary."

"She was electrocuted," Alison replied, after a moment.

"Sorry…?"

"In the salon. She was on her own. She had a late appointment. Her client left…and she was found the next morning by the manager…one of the hairdryers had a frayed cord and the coroner said there was evidence she had wet hands when she went to unplug it."

"Who was the client?"

"Mrs. Johnson. She works at the Co-op. The RCMP questioned her but she said Susan was alive when she left." Alison paused. "Do you think it's more than a coincidence? The hair dryer. Your Jacuzzi."

"If we didn't have Ben Quigley in common I'd have said it was just a coincidence. But I don't think that's true at all now. I honestly think someone's just tried to kill me."

#

Alison had mentioned Brenda Hubenko, who was working at Styles 'n' Smiles in 2013 when the festival promoter had had his wicked way with her.

I looked up the address then drove back into town. I'd thought of ringing first, but decided not to—my sense of trust was deteriorating, and I was beginning to think it would be better just to show up and ask questions, rather than warn people I was coming.

I'd guessed Brenda was still working there, and I wasn't wrong. The receptionist pointed her out to me—a young woman about Alison's age, with streaked black and bright blue hair tied up in a jaunty ponytail.

I sat in a chair in the waiting area, paging through magazines filled with pictures of models with hair styled in ways that would take two hours and crackerjack expertise with implements, sprays and gels to replicate, until Brenda had popped her customer under the dryer.

"Hi," she said, sitting in the chair beside me. "Wendy says you want to talk to me…?"

I told her who I was, and why I was in Peace River. I threw Ben's name into the mix, just to see how she'd react.

"Oh yeah," she said, thinking. "He was one of the performers at the festival. I remember."

"But you've heard nothing about him since?" I checked.

She shook her head, and I believed her.

Two women arrived for their appointments with other stylists, joining us in the waiting area.

"Is there somewhere more private…?" I asked.

"Come with me," Brenda said.

I followed her to the last chair in a row of six in front of a wall of mirrors. She invited me to sit down.

"Want a little trim while you're here?"

"A little," I allowed. I like my hair on the long side and somewhat untidy. I champion the look of the unkempt musical genius.

She reached for her scissors and a comb.

"Going kinda grey there," she said, pointing out something I'd begun to notice over the past year or two. "Maybe think about adding a little colour…?"

"Maybe not," I replied, humorously. I'm not a fan of what other musical geniuses have done in pursuit of eternal public youth. At best it looks unnatural against an aging face, at worst it's grotesque.

"You'd look good with blue streaks," Brenda said, and I think she actually meant it.

"Susan Collingwood used to work here."

"Yeah. She showed up in…" Brenda paused to think. "…2011. I remember because I was 19 and I was working at the hardware store and I came here to get my hair done and she was new. I got talking to her and told her I wasn't sure what to do with my life and she suggested going to an academy to get training in hair design…and I thought, that's a pretty good deal, so I did."

"So Susan was responsible for your career choice."

"Yup," said Brenda, snipping a little too much off the bits of hair around my ears. She caught my wince in the mirror and went around to the back of my head where I couldn't see what she was doing.

"And did she ever say why she decided to move here from England?"

"I guess she came out to see her sister and she decided to stay."

Brenda obviously knew more than Alison.

"Who's her sister?"

"Miriam Bailey," Alison said.

"Miriam?" I said. "Miriam who makes mukluks and moccasins and regularly goes off her meds?"

"Yeah. That Miriam."

To say I was completely flabbergasted would have been an understatement.

I pulled out my phone and showed Brenda the obituary. "Marion Bailey," I said.

"Nope. That's gotta be a typo. It's definitely Miriam."

"But Miriam doesn't have an English accent."

"She never lived in England. She was born here. She grew up here. She got her welding papers and used to work over at Haney's Machine Shop. I think she had to quit when...you know..."

Brenda made a hand gesture in the mirror, circling her pointer finger around the side of her head.

"I know," I said. "I saw her at the Riverfront Cafe the other day."

I paused. There was no way Alison didn't know about Susan being Miriam's sister. No way on earth.

"Did Susan and Miriam have the same parents?" I asked, looking again at the obituary.

"I think they had the same father." I didn't know what Brenda was doing around the back of my collar but I suddenly felt a draft. "Susan's mom moved to Puerto Vallarta and married a Mexican guy. Miriam's mom was Joanne. Joanne and Sam Bailey."

"They died in a car accident," I said.

"Yeah, about ten years ago. They hit some black ice on the highway and spun out into a truck coming the other way."

I shivered. I'd rescued my car—and myself—just in time. Another three seconds…

"Was this common knowledge in town?" I asked.

"You mean about Susan and Miriam?"

"I do."

"Pretty much everyone knew," Brenda shrugged.

She was making a move on the hair that was usually combed down over my forehead in a carefully dishevelled fringe.

"Thank you," I said, sliding out of the chair. "You've been incredibly helpful."

I took out my wallet.

"How much do I owe you for the trim?"

"On the house," Brenda said, beaming. "I just love your accent."

I left her a generous tip anyway. And then I drove over to the Riverview Cafe and sat down with a cup of coffee and slice of cheesecake and I rang Alison.

"I just didn't make the connection, Jason. I'm sorry."

"You know everyone in town," I said. "How could you not know that Susan was Miriam's sister? And especially when Susan died—you'd have seen her obituary. You work at the newspaper."

"I wasn't working at the *Rocket* back then. I was still at university in Edmonton. I lived in Edmonton.

I only came home so I could get some extra money working at the hotel over the summer. There was a lot of stuff I missed."

I wanted to believe Alison. Her explanation was plausible. I rang off and checked the time on my phone. It was two in the afternoon and my stomach, which still insisted I was in London, was demanding to know why I'd neglected to offer it both lunch and dinner.

I ordered an immense hamburger topped with bacon and ham and cheese and pickles, and an equally immense plate of chips with gravy, and another cup of coffee. And while I waited for it all to be delivered to my table, I logged into the Riverview's free Wi-Fi and did another search for Ben Quigley's name.

I landed on a page that a fan had put together, that I'd glanced over previously but not really paid much attention to.

I'm not fond of fan websites as a general rule, although some of them are exceptionally well done and outshine the official attempts. I just find it a bit tedious when they get into obscure arguments about the weight of the strings that were used on different guitars in different versions of songs, and it's all based on opinion and conjecture with no input at all from the artists.

This wasn't one of those sites. It was just facts, neatly compiled and presented in an uncomplicated way, with a few photos and scans of program covers added in to break up the text.

This particular fan had tried to put together a reconstruction of Ben's "lost years". There were several periods in question: 1983, 1992, and 2001.

In 1983 Ben had trekked to India and found enlightenment.

In 2001 he decamped to Spain and spent about six months drinking red wine, sleeping on the beach, and attempting to write songs.

Nobody was sure where he disappeared to in 1992 but this fan had tracked down some photos which claimed to show Ben in Alaska, and also in San Francisco. And there was a scan of a letter from another follower who'd reported she'd definitely met Ben in a bar in Ensenada, Mexico, where he'd been downing shots of tequila and telling outrageous jokes.

There was a section containing random pictures that had been collected over the years. I looked them over…and then stopped.

There was one of Ben, standing between two women. I'd have passed right over it, dismissing it as one of those photos fans often ask celebrities to pose for.

But I recognized one of the women. And the explanation underneath confirmed it.

Ben with Miriam Bailey and Susan Collingwood in Newcastle, England, April 2009.

I saved the photo to my phone, and then I sent it to Alison, along with the caption.

And then I rang her.

"They both knew Ben."

"They'd both met him," Alison corrected. "It doesn't prove they both knew him."

"Where's Miriam likely to be right now, do you know?"

"I guess she's probably at home."

"Good. I want to have a word with her. I'd like to ask her about Susan. And Ben."

"Do you want me to come with you?"

"That might be a good idea," I said.

"I'm just going into an editorial meeting. Can you wait a couple of hours?"

"No," I said. "I can't. How do I get to her house?"

#

The old farm where Miriam lived turned out to involve a series of directions that included the Number 2 highway, the bridge over the river, and a half hour cross-country journey along roads with three-digit numbers and descriptors like Range, Township and Pulp Mill.

The actual drive started out on a fairly large highway which turned into a much smaller highway, and then another road that stopped being paved two kilometres past the intersection and reverted to slippery, ice-covered gravel.

There weren't a lot of other cars but the ones I did meet were coming my way at a good clip. I pulled over to the side of the road and waited until they'd gone past, terrified that my lack of winter driving skills would land me upside down in one of the snow-filled ditches.

To reach Miriam's house I had to turn off the small gravel road and onto what was basically a lane which hadn't been plowed. I directed my car into a pair of ruts that had been dug into the snow by others with better tires than mine, and then, following Alison's instructions, turned into the first clearing and drove into the yard.

I wasn't sure what I was expecting. My experience with old rural houses is largely limited to England, everything ancient and rambling, stone and flint and ivy and wildflowers, fields of woolly lambs and chickens pecking at pebbles.

Miriam's house was, without a doubt, very old. It belonged to another era, possibly the early years of the 20th century, and had been built to accommodate a very large family. It was square, and made of wood, and it had two main floors and a further half floor with two windows up in the roof. It was perched on top of a concrete base, which was mostly buried in the ground, and it had a porch, which was enclosed, and a tall brick chimney, and the whole of it was clad in wooden siding and painted a very nondescript and faded grey.

I didn't see Miriam's truck.

I got out of the car.

It was an extremely tidy yard. There was a large garage off to the right, and off to the left, what looked like a workshop and a couple of large storage buildings made out of wood and in the shape of silos. I could see a ragged hole punched into the side of one of the silos, and leading away from it, a trail of what looked like pieces of animal fur scattered over the snow.

The deer and moose hides, I reasoned, although in my imagination I'd pictured them as being tanned and cleaned of all residual hair. These pieces of hide were clean but still had the hair intact, and as I bent down to examine one of them I was struck by how beautiful the coarse hairs were, and how colourful: light brown, and black, and white. These hide pieces wouldn't have been very satisfying to the bear—or whatever it was—more like a dog's chew-toy—an appetizer—than anything else.

As I stood up, I saw that there were more pieces of animal further away, scattered haphazardly and disappearing into the trees. I saw raw meat, red against the brilliant white snow, and sinew and muscle and bone as well as skin and hair. This was the real thing. The recently eviscerated carcass of something living and unfortunate enough to have become something's dinner.

I had a thought, which was actually quite terrifying. What if the bear—or whatever it was— was still about? What if I was on the menu as dessert?

I scanned the pine trees, the bare poplars and birch and scrubby little bushes that grew around the perimeter of the yard, and quickly worked out my plan of escape if a large, hulking carnivore should suddenly appear and lurch in my direction. The car was my first refuge but it was over there by the house and I was up here by the wooden silos…and the only other shelter I could see was the workshop.

The door wasn't locked. I poked my head inside and flicked on the light and saw a clutter of cutting and sewing machines which I supposed Miriam used to fashion the animal hides into the things she sold in the shop and at the country fairs. I saw clamps and presses and the sorts of tools you'd imagine someone would need to keep a rural farmhouse in good running order.

I switched the light off and closed the door securely and, after checking again for hungry wildlife, made a beeline back to my car.

I sat in the driver's seat for a couple of minutes, studying the house. I had to admit it did look a bit spooky. I'm not like Alison—I do actually believe in ghosts, largely because of an intensely personal experience I had aboard the *Sapphire* before she went to the bottom of the ocean. I believe in guardian angels, too. And people who are highly intuitive and psychic. Not the ones who charge you a small fortune for vaguely provable predictions and observations that anyone could do with a modicum of instinct about human nature. The ones who quietly live amongst us, who meet you by accident and touch your arm and tell you things about yourself they couldn't possibly have looked up, or specific things they know will happen…and then they do.

Well.

There was still no sign of Miriam.

I briefly debated the ethics of what I was about to do.

I'd come this far. And it was going to be a long, slippery drive back to town with nothing to show for the effort.

I got out of the car and climbed up the steps to the porch, and knocked.

Nothing. Of course. But formalities needed to be observed.

The porch door wasn't locked. I let myself in, and tried the main door. That one wasn't locked either. I knocked again.

And again, nothing. Dead silence. No sounds from within. No giveaway rustles or footsteps or creaks or slams.

I let myself inside.

I knew I was breaking the law. And there would be consequences if I was caught.

But I had a suspicion, and I needed to know.

I went down to the very bottom of the house—the cellar—which was dug into the earth and had unfinished concrete walls and contained a monstrosity of a metal octopus with insulated pipes sprouting out of its sides and disappearing up into the wooden ceiling. I studied it by the light thrown from my mobile. Some kind of ancient oil furnace, I assumed, judging by the tank standing nearby. Hulking and creepy, and making the cellar altogether unwelcoming.

I swept my light around the entire perimeter and

across the concrete floor. The only other occupants of the cellar were an old-fashioned washing machine with a round tub, and a hand-cranked mangle.

I might have stepped back into another century.

It certainly smelled like something that had been buried in another century. Dank and earthy and not altogether pleasant. The kind of smell that made me think of a freshly-opened tomb.

I shivered, and climbed back up the rickety wooden steps to the kitchen, then walked through to the front of the house, to check again for Miriam's truck.

Still no sign of her.

The rest of the house could have come straight out of the beginnings of the last century as well. I could see there had been some attempts at modernization—a new tile floor in the kitchen and newish-looking cabinets. But the windows and doors looked as if they'd been installed when the house was built, and all of the original hardwood flooring was still in place.

I'm not sure what I'd been expecting, knowing that Miriam had grown up in this house and that she was living there now and had been for some years. Perhaps I'd anticipated the detritus of a hoarder— cardboard boxes filled with inconceivable collections, newspapers, magazines, Christmas ornaments, empty bottles. I once had an aunt who kept everything she'd ever been given or bought, "just in case". Her house had caught fire and she'd perished, largely because the firefighters had to negotiate past sixty years of *The Times* to locate her.

Miriam was not a hoarder. In fact, if I had to categorize her, I'd have said she was fastidiously clean. The kitchen, the living and dining rooms, the big main bedroom and the front hall, all on the main floor, were spotless.

I went upstairs to the second floor, where there were four more bedrooms, none of which contained beds, and a big old-fashioned bathroom, with an animal-pawed tub and a pedestal sink and a newer-looking toilet. All of those rooms were clean and tidy too.

Miriam had met Ben before. Susan had met Ben at the same time, and then two years after that she'd moved to Peace River to be close to her sister. And two years after that Ben had come to Peace River too. Had Ben met both of them again while he was here?

I checked the yard in front of the house again, looking down through one of the front bedroom windows, taking care that I couldn't be seen.

No sign of the battered, rusty truck.

As I walked out of the bedroom, I spotted a tiny, narrow staircase leading up from the landing, and then around, and up again, to what I assumed was the half floor with the two little windows in the roof.

I went up the stairs, only to find my way blocked at the top by a door, which was locked.

None of the other doors in the house were locked. They weren't even closed.

Why this one?

It was one of those things with an upright keyhole below the knob, an original as old as the house.

I know how to pick locks. It's a skill I learned a long time ago, though I'm not sure it would be wise to share how and why and who taught me.

I found a wire clothes hanger in one of the bedroom cupboards downstairs, bent it the way I wanted it, and had the door open in a couple of seconds.

What I discovered inside the little room literally took my breath away.

It was a shrine, and it was dedicated to Ben Quigley.

Figgis Green had a colour they used for all their marketing—a really distinctive shade of moss green they adopted as their own. It showed up on all their album covers, in their stage lighting, even in some of the group members' clothes when they were performing. My mum had a Figgis Green hat she sometimes popped on in the second half of their gigs. My dad had a Figgis Green vest.

The walls of the shrine to Ben were painted Figgis Green. And all around the little room were things a fan would collect: concert posters and photos—Ben alone, Ben with Figgis Green, Ben as an opening act for somebody else, Ben headlining, Ben featured at Disturbing the Peace.

On little wooden tables and stools were programs from all of those gigs. And CD's, and cassettes, and vinyl records. Newspaper clippings—stories, ads, photos…a backstage pass to the music festival, hanging on a lanyard.

A framed photo of Ben as a child, with his mum. And two more—Ben as a teenager, staring the camera down.

Stuff you could buy at a couple of Figgis Green reunion concerts that were put together before my dad died—t-shirts, key rings, mugs, pins, fridge magnets.

A mike on a stand, and a portable Marshall amp.

Some clothes—were they Ben's? Purple velvet trousers and a lilac shirt…nailed to the wall as if Ben had been wearing them.

And a guitar. Electric. Ben's. I knew it was his. Absolutely and without any doubt whatsoever.

Unfortunately, I'd turned my back to the attic door.

Unfortunately, as I was standing there, staring at Ben's Lake Placid Blue Fender Strat, flabbergasted, someone came up behind me and coshed me over the head with something very big and very heavy.

The last thing I recalled was collapsing onto the floor. And then everything went very black.

#

I have only fleeting memories of what happened next, like curtains opening intermittently to let in a rush of fresh air and sun, then flinging shut again, plunging me back into darkness.

I was lying on my side on the floor, which smelled

like wet wood and dirt. I couldn't move my arms or legs, and I wasn't sure why, until I realized my hands were fastened behind my back, and my ankles were tied together. It didn't feel like rope—more like thick wire, with no give.

My head was pounding and the pain was more intense than the worst migraine I could ever recall. I risked opening my eyes, and once everything had stopped spinning, I recognized where I was: Miriam's workshop.

Various other parts of me were starting to hurt now…knees and elbows and ribs…it felt like I'd been dragged down the stairs and across the floor and then across the yard through the snow. The legs of my jeans were wet. I'd unzipped my jacket when I'd gone inside the house, and there were places on my t-shirt that were soaking, where snow had obviously been scooped up and melted. There was something in my mouth…a piece of a twig. I coughed it out, and heard someone swear: a woman.

"Shit. Why are you awake?"

It was Miriam. If I shifted a little, I could just see her standing at the wooden table, fiddling with something.

I thought it best not to answer. I had no idea what her state of mind was, and if she was the one who'd bashed me over the head and dragged me outside and tied me up, I wasn't sure what else she was capable of.

"Anyway," she continued, conversationally, "I've figured out a way to get rid of you for good. I could shoot you. I have a gun. I keep it handy because of the bears. But I wouldn't want the bears to eat the shot. It's not good for them."

I stayed silent. I couldn't work my hands free. The wire was cutting into my wrists.

"Nobody'll ever find your body if I leave you in the trees. Well…maybe the bears. In the spring."

She was wearing a protective jacket and heavy lace-up boots with thick rubber soles. There was a weird-looking helmet on the table beside a pair of leather gloves.

She carried a black and red piece of machinery over to me and put it on the floor. It looked like a portable Hoover. Except it had two electrical leads coming out of it with clamps on both ends.

"Still with me?" she said, bending down to look at my face.

"I don't have much choice," I said.

"This is the grounding wire and it gets attached to the leg of the table," she replied, helpfully, clamping it onto the waistband of my jeans.

She held up the other lead.

"This is where you put the rod. And then after you flip the switch, you draw the rod along your base metal, the electric arc melts the rod, and you have a perfect weld."

She placed a slender metallic stick into the clamp on the second lead.

"I'm really proud of my welding ticket. Woman of many talents, me. Also have my electrician's papers. I can fix anything."

She bent down again, and tapped my nose with the welding rod.

"I can fix you."

"You electrocuted Susan," I said. I could hear my heart pounding.

"Nothing to connect me to that," Miriam replied. She carried the power cord to an outlet in the wall, and plugged it in.

"And you did something to my Jacuzzi."

"Yeah, that didn't work, did it? Too bad. Nothing to connect me to that, either."

"Why Susan?"

"She had to go."

"Why? And what happened to Ben?"

Miriam didn't answer. She came back to the welding machine, and, bending down, switched it on.

She aimed the rod at my forehead between my eyes. I couldn't move my head. I was petrified. My heartbeat was deafening. I realized it might possibly be the very last thing I would ever hear. I think I closed my eyes. The black curtain was coming down again. I think I heard her laugh and then—

"Mom!" a woman's voice screamed. "Mom! No! Don't!"

I struggled back to consciousness and saw a hand yank the power cord out of the wall.

"He was going to spoil everything!" Miriam yelled.

"Are you ok, Jason?"

It was Alison, and she was kneeling beside me on the floor.

And there was an RCMP officer with her, and he

was telling Miriam he was arresting her for attempted murder and she had the right to right to retain and instruct counsel without delay and that she need not say anything but anything she did or said might be used as evidence and did she understand?

#

Alison's best friend Karen—Dr. Giroux—was the doctor at the Peace River Community Health Centre when I arrived at Emergency. Alison drove me there in her Explorer, leaving mine parked in Miriam's yard, plugged into a long extension cord coming out of the garage.

"We'll pick it up later," she said.

To be honest, I was having trouble taking it all in. What I'd discovered in the attic at Miriam's house. What had nearly just happened to me in the workshop. The fact that Alison was Miriam's daughter. The other fact that Alison had been lying to me all along. And if not lying, then being extremely economical with the truth.

And if Miriam had created that shrine in the attic…what had happened to Ben?

Dr. Giroux checked me over, discovering all of the bruises that had been caused by Miriam bumping me down several flights of stairs and across the yard to the workshop. Nothing broken, although she did express surprise that Miriam had been able to drag me that far by herself.

"She has a welding ticket," I said. "She's capable of anything."

Dr. Giroux laughed. And, after examining my head, diagnosed a concussion, suggested I rest and not do anything strenuous or which required my brain to function properly, and further recommended I see my own doctor when I was back in London.

"Is there someone here who can keep an eye on you for the next twenty-four hours? Just to make sure your symptoms don't get any worse?"

"No," I said.

"Alison's in the waiting room. She's offered to let you stay with her…"

"No thanks," I said. "I'll ring someone in England."

"Are you sure…?"

"I'm sure," I said.

And so I was discharged, with the promise that I'd give Dom or my mum the number for the hospital, and if I sounded confused or not at all well when I called them to check in, they'd be in touch immediately.

Alison drove me back to my hotel, and then, because it was dark and I'd completely lost track of the time and I was starving, she walked across to the steak place and brought back a burger and chips.

"And I'll make us some coffee," she decided, filling up the little kettle beside the microwave.

I was sitting on the bed, attempting to eat the

burger without causing an explosion of condiments.

"You need a bib," she said, tucking a paper napkin into the collar of my t-shirt, a gesture I found uncommonly irritating.

"Where's Ben?" I said.

"I don't know," Alison said. "And that's the truth. When he came here for the festival, he wanted to meet mom. Mom told him Susan was here too, but he didn't want to see her."

"Did the meeting happen?"

Alison nodded. "The day after the festival. She went to his hotel room. And then…after that…he disappeared."

"You neglected to mention Miriam's your mother. Different last names notwithstanding."

"When I was born my mom was dating a trucker named Seth McCall. So she put him down as my dad on my birth certificate. He didn't stick around for too long after that. Mom raised me alone."

"And you lied about not knowing Miriam and Susan were sisters."

"I did," she admitted. "I'm sorry."

"Why?"

"I just…didn't want you to make the connection."

"Why?" I asked again.

Alison didn't answer. She went back to the little kitchen alcove to make two mugs of instant coffee. "Cream and sugar?"

"Both," I said. "I asked your mother what had happened to Susan, and she said Susan had to go. What did she mean?"

Again, Alison didn't answer. She carried the two mugs back to the bedside table and dragged a chair over and sat down.

"Is it possible your mum might have had something to do with Susan's death?"

Alison nodded. Reluctantly. "But I don't know. And I don't think anyone ever will. And that's the truth, Jason."

"So this was all about protecting her?"

Again, a nod.

I didn't believe her.

"Did you know that Susan once tried to claim that Ben Quigley was her father?"

"I didn't until she moved here. She didn't want to accept the DNA results."

"They're not usually wrong," I said. "Why did she decide to come to Peace River?"

Alison drank her coffee. And then: "Because mom told her she'd had an affair with Ben in 1992."

"That doesn't seem like something that would cause me to pack up everything and relocate halfway around the world. Is it true?"

Alison nodded. "He was in Alaska. He bought a car and drove down through Yukon and the Northwest Territories and he ended up here."

"Do you know about the room in your mum's attic that has all Ben's things in it?"

"No," Alison said, looking genuinely surprised.

"I'll show it to you when we go back tomorrow for my car," I said. "I was looking at it when your mum bashed me over the head. Obviously something she didn't want me to see."

"Susan was obsessed with Ben. Completely over the top obsessed."

"You're suggesting that's Susan's work, not your mum's?"

"She was living in the house with mom."

"So…not in an apartment in downtown Peace River, then. Another lie."

"I'm sorry."

"So you say."

Alison stood up.

"I have to go. Gord's going to let me talk to mom. Her mental state really isn't very good these days."

"You could have fooled me," I said. "Gord would be the RCMP officer you showed up with earlier…?"

"Corporal Richards. I tried calling you after my editorial meeting and your phone went to messaging. Three times in a row. I got worried and asked him to come out to mom's house with me."

"Thanks," I said. "What did your mum mean when she said I was going to spoil everything?"

"I don't know, Jason. I'll ask her."

I didn't get up off the bed and she let herself out of the room.

I abandoned the burger and finished my coffee and then gave Dom a ring. It was the middle of the night over there, but I needed to talk to someone I loved and trusted and who wasn't genetically and emotionally linked to a psychotic killer.

#

I slept surprisingly well.

It was only nine o'clock when I woke up, and they were still serving eggs and toast and pancakes in the breakfast room. I showered and shaved and got dressed and went downstairs to investigate.

An hour later Alison was waiting for me outside the hotel in her Explorer, engine running and heat blowing full blast inside.

She was silent all the way out to the farm. I'd debated asking Corporal Gord to accompany us, but reasoned if Alison had wanted to do anything bad to me, she'd already had two opportunities, and she wasn't likely to risk it with the Peace River RCMP Detachment's radar already focused on her mum.

Alison parked the Explorer next to my car, and we got out.

"Come with me," I said.

I took her inside the house and up the stairs to the attic.

"Wow," she said, as I opened the door.

Her reaction was genuine. She'd really had no idea.

She walked around, looking at the posters and souvenirs, pausing at the photos someone had taken of Ben onstage at the festival.

"I remember that," she said, thoughtfully.

"I think," I said, "that this is your mum's shrine to Ben, not Susan's. And I think that Susan was obsessed with him, yes, but that the two of them were competing for his attention. And I think that Susan got in the way and she had to go."

Alison was looking at me.

"If this was Susan's shrine," I said, "why would your mum have kept it intact like this, all locked up and obviously well-cared for? I don't see any dust. I don't see any cobwebs. Do you?"

Alison shook her head.

I stopped in front of Ben's electric guitar, the Lake Placid Blue Fender Strat that my dad had bought for him when he'd joined Figgis Green. It was lying on a table in its hard travelling case, the lid propped open.

"That's the guitar in that photo from the festival."

I looked around the long, narrow room.

"What?" Alison said.

"Where's the other one?" I said, indicating the picture next to the one of Ben with the Strat. It had also been taken onstage—Ben was wearing the same clothes in both, the purple velvet trousers and lilac shirt that were tacked to the wall on the opposite side of the room. But in the second photo he was playing a Gibson acoustic worth about three thousand quid. "He came here with two guitars—I know that for a fact. Ben wouldn't leave one behind and take the other. Where's the Gibson?"

I walked to the other end of the room, where a single window overlooked the rear of the yard. It was a jumble of bare-branched poplars, birch and aspens and evergreen spruces and pines. I could see footsteps in the snow, tracking back into the undergrowth.

"What's through there?" I said.

Alison came to look.

"Just an old wooden outhouse," she said. "It was built the same time as this place, before they got plumbing and electricity."

But something else had caught my eye.

"I'm going downstairs," I said.

It was indeed an old, derelict wooden outhouse, a little shack built over a dug-out cesspit.

But that wasn't what I'd seen.

What I'd seen was a glimpse of something orange, which upon closer inspection turned out to be an outdoor extension cord, the same sort of heavy-duty, weatherproof cord that had come with my rented car. It was buried under a drift, and had only come to light because someone had trodden on it, their boot displacing the dry snow so it was exposed.

I pulled up the cord and followed it all the way back to the house. It was plugged into an outlet in the wall above one of the cellar windows.

"What's at the other end?" I asked Alison.

Alison shook her head. "No idea."

"What else is in the trees?"

"Just a couple of old log cabins the original homesteaders built. They're everywhere. Most of them were abandoned during the Depression."

I pulled the cord up out of the snow and followed it into the woods, stepping over fallen trunks and dry brittle twigs. Was this where Miriam had planned on leaving my body for the bears, once it had been charred beyond recognition by her welding arc?

The orange cord—and the footsteps in the snow—led to a small clearing in the trees, and to one of two rough-hewn cabins. The first had collapsed in on itself, its roof gone and its walls surrendering to gravity. The second was in better shape, its roof intact, its walls solid, the mud chinking between the horizontal axe-and-saw-cut logs still in place.

There was one window and one door. The window had unbroken glass in it, and was covered by a curtain on the inside. The door was new, and kept shut with a heavy-duty latch and an equally formidable padlock. The orange extension cord disappeared inside the cabin through a gap in the logs.

"Mom's got a bolt-cutter in the workshop," Alison said.

She ran back through the trees while I waited at the cabin. I listened at the window. Nothing. I hammered on the door with my fist, and then shouted Ben's name.

Was that a groan? Or my imagination?

Alison was back with a huge bolt-cutter. I got the jaws onto the shackle of the padlock and used all of my strength to lever the handles together. The shackle snapped. I tossed the padlock into the snow and kicked open the door.

The stench was overwhelming.

By the light from the opening I saw an earthen

floor covered in feces and pooled liquid which could only have been urine. There were three plastic buckets, one filled with a stinking brown sludge, the second overflowing with more urine, a third containing about an inch of clean water.

I saw the orange extension cord, and what it was plugged into: a portable electric heater, which was switched to On, but which was obviously broken as there wasn't any warmth coming from it.

There were dirty rags strewn everywhere, which I saw were actually clothes—trousers and shirts and socks. There was an old armchair which looked mouse-gnawed and mildewed, and a bed which was made up of two torn and stained mattresses stacked one on top of the other. On top of the bed was a dishevelled mound of blankets and ragged quilts. Beside the bed, on the floor, were remnants of food—bones which had been gnawed clean.

There was a lean-to built onto the back of the cabin which contained a toilet, but the toilet was as foul as the floor and the buckets.

And then I caught sight of it: Ben's Gibson acoustic six-string, stood up in the far corner, away from the muck and the rubbish, undamaged, intact.

I looked at Alison, who was holding her scarf over her nose and mouth because of the stench. She looked back at me, and I could see the hopelessness in her eyes. Then her eyes shifted to the mattresses behind me.

I turned around. The mound of filthy blankets was moving. A thin white hand, almost skeletal, reached out to us, and a weak, raspy voice whispered: "Please…will you help me…"

#

Ben had been shackled to the rear wall of the cabin with a steel cuff around his ankle and a chain that went outside through a gap in the logs and was welded around a substantial tree trunk. The cuff was fastened with two rivets, and the chain was long enough to allow him to go to into the lean-to at the back, and to walk halfway through the cabin at the front. But the door and the window were out of reach.

He was barely alive, his thin hair white and matted, a grizzled beard covering his face. He was shivering uncontrollably with the cold, and he was starving, thirsty, dirty and very very ill.

I hacked the chain with the bolt-cutters and we carried Ben out of the cabin and through the trees to the house, where we laid him on a sofa in the living room and fetched pillows and blankets from a bedroom and food and a hot drink from the kitchen. And then, while Alison rang Corporal Gord and Dr. Giroux, I walked through the trees and, holding my breath, retrieved Ben's guitar from the far corner of the cabin.

"I'm so sorry," Alison was saying, when I got back. "I had no idea, Ben. I truly didn't know."

"She kept me in food, when she felt like it," Ben whispered. "And water. And once or twice a month…hot water. So I could wash. And guitar strings. She always brought me fresh guitar strings." He shook his head. "Madwoman."

"You're safe now," I said.

Ben peered at me. "Jason…?"

"Your knight in shining armour," Alison said, kneeling down beside the sofa. "If it hadn't been for his persistence, I don't think you'd have been found."

Ben took my hand, and hers, and kissed them both, tenderly.

"Thank you," he said. "Thank you."

PART THREE

It was a special night at The Blue Devil. Ben Quigley was in the house. My fellow bandmates— Ken, Dave and Rudy—tenor sax, organ and drums—were just slightly shy of being in awe. None of them had ever met Ben before, but they all could recount what kind of influence, however small, his playing had made on their careers.

After our last set was done—after I'd popped outside for a quick smoke (I'm trying to quit now, I seriously am, I've even bought one of those self-help books)—we joined Ben at the table I'd reserved. It was a bit crowded, but the audience had thinned out a little by then so we moved a second table over and rearranged ourselves. They didn't have to, but out of respect for Ben's new vow of sobriety, nobody was drinking. We ordered another round of posh fizzy water and colourful non-alcoholic concoctions from Charmaine, our bartending wizard, and Ben repeated to us what he'd told the journos who were clamouring for exclusives…how, after a night of unparalleled drinking, he'd passed out and woken up Miriam's prisoner in a ramshackle log cabin. How he'd no idea where he was being kept, and no idea what day it was, and how he'd eventually lost track of all of the days and the nights, the weeks, the months, the years. How Miriam had treated him with passionate devotion interspersed with unfathomable cruelty—dependant upon whether or not she was taking her medications—and how he'd survived the isolation and the hopelessness by retreating deep into his imagination for days at a time, invoking a behaviour a psychologist at the University of Haifa had helpfully defined as "Maladaptive Daydreaming" or "Daydreaming Disorder."

Both terms were now trending on social media.

He'd got back to London before his mum had passed away. I'd found his passport—still valid—in the artefacts in Miriam's attic, and after he'd been treated at the hospital in Grande Prairie, I'd made sure he was flown home Business Class, with all of its amenities: the pillow, the duvet, the toiletry kit, the private pod and the chef-inspired meals. Edith Quigley had died surrounded by love, with Ben holding her hand.

I cried. And I'm not uncomfortable telling you that.

There was one tabloid reporter who'd excelled in her intrusiveness and had flown with a photographer to Peace River to take lurid pictures of the log cabin and to interview anyone who was willing to voice an opinion about Miriam, who was facing a myriad of charges. This reporter also raised the question of Alison's parentage, and had gone so far as to speculate about the months that Ben had been in Peace River having an affair with Miriam, and Alison's subsequent birth date.

A DNA test was in the offing. Alison had agreed. Ben had agreed What they had not agreed to was making the results public. It was, they said, something they both wished to keep private. And I completely understood. Though I suspected Alison would share the details with me regardless.

Dom had put aside his distaste for jazz and had also joined us for the evening. Ken, Dave and Rudy were practising professional reserve in Ben's presence. Dom had no such constraints and his esteem knew no bounds. He had yet to convince Ben to let him do a biopic…but Dom can be very persuasive, and I reckoned within a few days he'd win him over.

"I liked that last tune you did," Dom said to me, as I sat down.

"Thank you very much," I replied. "Coming from you this is high praise indeed. Did you recognize it?"

Dom shook his head, puzzled.

Ben knew it. Figgis Green's best known song, a catchy folky pop thing about a faithless suitor and his careworn lady, tormented hearts, lessons learned and a really fortunate ending. *Roving Minstrel.* I'd jazzed it up and presented it as an instrumental in an altogether different key.

Because of the array of lights aimed at the stage while I was playing, I couldn't see Ben's reaction, but I knew he was appreciative. And there was a lot of applause when we finished, the loudest coming from his table.

As our server brought our drinks over from the bar, someone else from my past decided to surface.

"Sal!" I said. "I didn't know you were in the audience!"

It had been five years since I'd last seen Sally Jones. I was confined to a hospital bed aboard the *Star Amethyst*, having just been plucked from an inflatable life raft in the middle of the ocean after the *Sapphire* had gone down. Sally was Captain Callico's secretary. I'd lost track of her after that.

"Still on the ships?" I asked, grabbing a chair so she could sit down. She looked good—a little bit older, a little bit of grey in her hair, her figure reminding me a little bit more of my mum. We'd loved one another as friends aboard the *Sapphire*; I'd have married her in a minute, if she'd asked.

"God no," she said. "I've been working ashore."

"Anything exciting?"

"Hotel admin," she said, with a shrug. "And I tried StarSea Corporate in Southampton for a while but it didn't really suit me. I can't seem to settle."

"I'm the same," I said. It was true—it's an affliction all of us who've worked at sea share. It's difficult to get used to a life that isn't in motion, the view from our bedroom windows never changing, day after day after day.

I introduced Sal to everyone at our two tables. She remembered Dom, who'd come aboard the *Sapphire* for a couple of weeks during his school break all those years ago.

"You've grown," she said. "Taller than your dad now."

"And twice as bright," I said, making him acutely uncomfortable.

"I read about your brilliant detective work tracking Ben down," she said, a little hesitantly. "And the thing is, Jason…I was wondering…if you'd consider helping me sort out a problem. I'd be willing to pay you, of course…"

ABOUT THE AUTHOR

Winona Kent was born in London, England. She immigrated to Canada with her parents at age 3, and grew up in Regina, Saskatchewan, where she received her BA in English from the University of Regina. After settling in Vancouver, she graduated from UBC with an MFA in Creative Writing. More recently, she received her diploma in Writing for Screen and TV from Vancouver Film School.

Winona has been a temporary secretary, a travel agent and the Managing Editor of a literary magazine. Her writing breakthrough came many years ago when she won First Prize in the Flare Magazine Fiction Contest with her short story about an all-night radio newsman, *Tower of Power*. More short stories followed, and then novels: *Skywatcher*, *The Cilla Rose Affair*, *Cold Play*, *Persistence of Memory* and *In Loving Memory*. Winona's sixth novel, *Marianne's Memory*, will be published in 2018.

Winona currently lives in Vancouver and works as a Graduate Programs Assistant at the University of British Columbia.

Please visit Winona's website at www.winonakent.com for more information.

Made in the USA
Columbia, SC
28 February 2024